OLD FRIENDS

A FEIWEL AND FRIENDS BOOK
An imprint of Macmillan Publishing Group, LLC
120 Broadway, New York, NY 10271
mackids.com

Library of Congress Cataloging-in-Publication
Data is available.

First edition, 2022
Book design by Carolyn Bull and Mike Burroughs
Digitally illustrated using Adobe Photoshop software and a drawing pen display
Feiwel and Friends logo designed by Filomena Tuosto
Printed in China by RR Donnelley Asia Printing Solutions Ltd.,
Dongguan City, Guangdong Province

ISBN 978-1-250-80138-8 (hardcover)
1   3   5   7   9   10   8   6   4   2

OLD FRIENDS

Margaret Aitken Illustrated by Lenny Wen

Feiwel and Friends · New York

For Stuart, Alexander, Ruaridh,
and James, who make my world as sweet as
berry apple crisp. —M.A.

For Fanny, Connie, and Daniel,
the best supporters in my life who accepted
me for who I am. —L.W.

Marjorie loved growing seeds into gardens, knitting cozy
creations, and curling up in front of her favorite baking show.
If only she could find someone who loved these things, too.
Someone like Granny.

The kids in the neighborhood were great. But none of the other kids got excited about yarn and yard work the way Marjorie did.

Baking Book for Kids

granny

SKETCH BOOK

Who could Marjorie ask for help
if her scones were sunken?
Or if her sweet peas got slugs?
Marjorie missed Granny so much.

Then one day, she saw a sign.

COMMUNITY CENTER

SENIOR CITIZEN FRIENDS GROUP
EVERY SATURDAY 10 AM
GARDENING
CRAFTING
BAKING
JOIN US FOR A CHA-CHA-CHA.
NEW MEMBERS WELCOME!

Marjorie had no clue what a cha-cha-cha was,
but she longed for a friend.

A friend who loved gardening, crafting, and baking—
the thought of it gave her a wonderful feeling.
Like she had just baked the world's most
delicious berry apple crisp!

So, on Saturday morning, Marjorie packed her
knitting needles and headed to the community center.
She was just about to enter when . . .

"Stop right there, young lady!
That's for seniors only! Kids club is that way."
Marjorie sighed. How would she find a friend now?

She walked and walked and walked some more.
She thought about Granny.
Granny didn't let knots in her knitting hold her back.
If Granny's cake didn't rise, she washed her bowls and started again.

Granny didn't give up easily . . . and neither would she!
Marjorie knew just what to do.
It was time for a cardigan camouflage!

Marjorie sprinkled some flour,
perched some glasses,

and with a few floral scarves knotted,
some lavender perfume spritzed,
and her Mom's woolly cardigan buttoned,
she was Undercover Granny!

Wearing her disguise, Marjorie sneaked past the receptionist and slowly opened the door . . .

There to welcome her was a friendly smile. "Hi, I'm Arthur."

Arthur showed Marjorie around and
introduced her to the group.

She learned a new knitting stitch from Patrick,

gathered the latest gardening tips from Betty,

and got a scrumptious new recipe from Jill.

Marjorie was having a blast with
her new friends until . . .

"It's that time you've all
been waiting for—
Let's cha-cha-cha!"

Marjorie slunk down in her chair.
Dancing was NOT for her.

She was about to make a quick exit
when she got stopped by a samba sidestep.
She tried to twist around the table . . .
but got trapped in a tango tangle.

Her break-dancing breakout
was a bust, so she'd just have to
give the cha-cha-cha a whirl.
1, 2, cha-cha-cha . . .
3, 4, cha-cha-cha . . .

Soon, Marjorie was tapping and twirling so much that she didn't notice . . .

the flour puffing,
her scarf slipping,
and her glasses sliding,

until . . . Oh, NO!

"Wait!" Arthur shouted. "Don't go!"
"I'm sorry." Marjorie sniffed.
"I just wanted to make new friends."

"You did!" said Arthur.
"But I'm . . . just a kid."
They both sat down.
"Can I tell you a secret?"

"On the outside we may look old, but on the inside,
we still feel like kids. Just like you."
Everyone agreed.

"I hope you'll share that new
knitting pattern," said Patrick.

"I'd love to hear more about
your roses," said Betty.

Jill chimed in,
"Can you help us learn
some new moves?'"

"Please stay," they all said.

Marjorie smiled. "I'd love to!"
Something told her
Granny was smiling, too.

And so, Marjorie became
the youngest member of the
Senior Citizen Friends Group.
Until . . .

Frank turned up.